Dear Parent:
Your child's love of readin

Every child learns to read in a different way an
speed. Some go back and forth between reading levels and read
favorite books again and again. Others read through each level in
order. You can help your young reader improve and become more
confident by encouraging his or her own interests and abilities. From
books your child reads with you to the first books he or she reads
alone, there are I Can Read Books for every stage of reading:

SHARED READING
Basic language, word repetition, and whimsical illustrations,
ideal for sharing with your emergent reader

BEGINNING READING
Short sentences, familiar words, and simple concepts
for children eager to read on their own

READING WITH HELP
Engaging stories, longer sentences, and language play
for developing readers

READING ALONE
Complex plots, challenging vocabulary, and high-interest topics
for the independent reader

ADVANCED READING
Short paragraphs, chapters, and exciting themes
for the perfect bridge to chapter books

I Can Read Books have introduced children to the joy of reading
since 1957. Featuring award-winning authors and illustrators and a
fabulous cast of beloved characters, I Can Read Books set the
standard for beginning readers.

A lifetime of discovery begins with the magical words **"I Can Read!"**

Visit www.icanread.com for information
on enriching your child's reading experience.

Walking with Dinosaurs: Friends Stick Together

www.harpercollinschildrens.com

Library of Congress catalog card number: 2013934068
ISBN 978-0-06-223286-1 (trade bdg.)—ISBN 978-0-06-223285-4 (pbk.)
Typography by Rick Farley

13 14 15 16 17 LP/WOR 10 9 8 7 6 5 4 3 2 1

First Edition

I Can Read!™

READING 2 WITH HELP

WALKING WITH DINOSAURS THE 3D MOVIE

Friends Stick Together

Adapted by Alexis Barad-Cutler

HARPER
An Imprint of HarperCollinsPublishers

A long time ago,
deep in the Arctic,
a group of baby dinosaurs
was born.

These were Pachyrhinosaurus,
large plant eaters with a big frill
on their necks.
The Pachyrhinosaurus spent
their early days inside a cozy nest.

Their mother watched over them.

The smallest in the nest was Patchi.

One day, Patchi wandered
away from the nest.
A clever dinosaur with feathers,
called a Troodon,
snatched him up and darted away!

Luckily, Patchi's father,
Bulldust, saved his son
and scared the Troodon off.

Patchi was hurt.

When he saw his shadow on the ground,

there was a shaft of light

shining through his frill.

The Troodon had taken a bite out of it,
leaving a large hole!

Patchi was a little bit clumsy
and extremely curious.

Scowler was one of Patchi's older brothers.
He was the largest and strongest
of all his brothers and sisters.

Patchi wanted to be
just like his father.
He watched Bulldust wrestle
with Scowler.
They were both much bigger than him.

Alex, an Alexornis, became friends
with Patchi.
Alex thought the young
Pachyrhinosaurus was special.
Alex rode on Patchi's frill
and ate the insects that landed there.

Patchi went to find another friend.
He followed a butterfly
into the woods.

When he got to a stream,
he noticed another
Pachyrhinosaurus by the water.
It was Juniper, a young female
his own age.

Patchi knew Juniper
would make a great friend.
The two friends
had many challenges to face.

They were separated from
their herds during
their first migration.

However, they were reunited
with the rest of their herds
at the Winter Ground.

Juniper went with her mother
while Patchi stayed with Scowler.

Patchi and Scowler grew up.
Scowler became one of
the strongest in the herd.

One day, while Patchi watched
the older Pachyrhinosaurus compete,
he noticed a familiar face.
It was Juniper.

Patchi was happy
to see his old friend.

The Pachyrhinosaurus
were ready to migrate again.
It was time to go
back to the nesting ground.

Just like their first migration,
Juniper and Patchi
faced many challenges.

The two friends helped
a young Pachyrhinosaurus
cross a frozen lake.

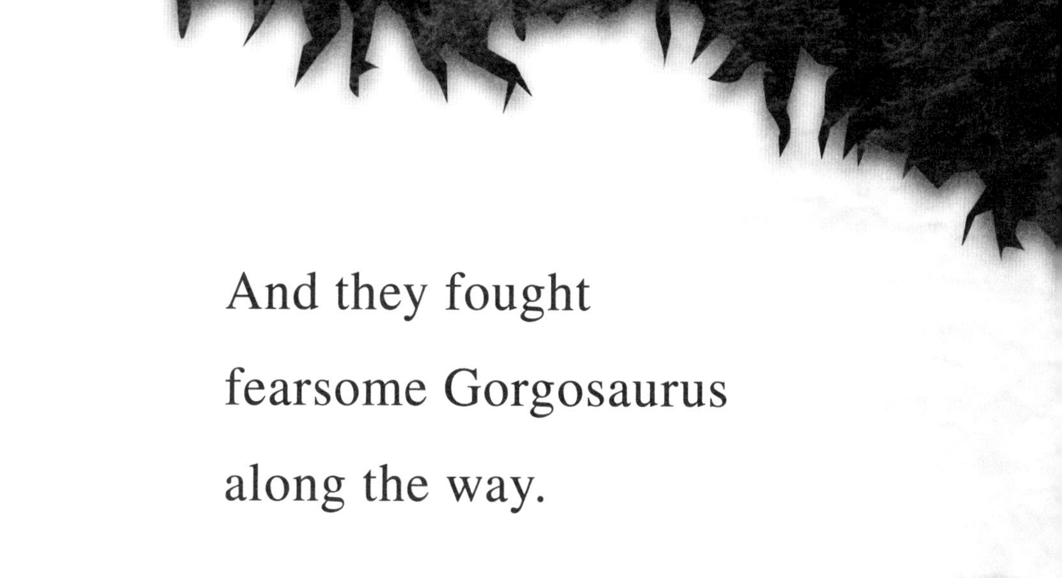

And they fought
fearsome Gorgosaurus
along the way.

Patchi and Juniper were best friends,
and together,
they made a great team.